Starring

Rufus

Lulu

Tucker

Stella

Mops

To the Sacred Heart
Kindergarten Class,

Have fun with
words!

♥

*To Arianna, Sophia,
Eliza, and Rich,
and in loving memory of Kim*

RUFUS AND FRIENDS
RHYME TIME

Traditional poems
extended and illustrated by

Iza Trapani

iɔi Charlesbridge

RUFUS AND FRIENDS
RHYME TIME

4

Come join us for a happy time.
Let's have some fun with words and rhyme.
The silly sounds that you will hear
Should make you smile from ear to ear.
These playful poems, fun and sweet,
Make for a great tongue-twisting treat!
We took old rhymes and added new,
And now we'll act them out for you!

Betty Botter

Betty Botter bought some butter,
But she said, "The butter's bitter.
If I put it in my batter,
It will make my batter bitter.
But a bit of better butter . . .
That would make my batter better."

If a bit of better butter
Would make Betty's batter better,
Then a bunch of better butter
Would be even better yetter!
So she bought a bunch of butter,
Which was better for her batter,
And that made Betty Botter
A much gladder butter adder.

Then she added all the butter,
First one batch and then another.
And another, and another,
Till along came Betty's mother,
Which made Betty Botter flutter.
(She would hear about the clutter.)

Betty beat the buttered batter.
Pitter patter, pitter patter.
Spatter, splatter, scatter batter.
Splattered one way, then another.

7

Splat! It landed on her mother!

From Wibbleton to Wobbleton

From Wibbleton to Wobbleton is fifteen miles.

From Wobbleton to Wibbleton is fifteen miles.

From Wibbleton to Wobbleton,

From Wobbleton to Wibbleton,

From Wibbleton to Wobbleton is fifteen miles.

From Wiggleton to Waggleton is fifteen miles.

From Waggleton to Wiggleton is fifteen miles.

From Wiggleton to Wobbleton,

From Waggleton to Wibbleton,

From Wibbleton to Wiggleton,

From Wobbleton to Waggleton,

From Wibbleton to Wobbleton is fifteen miles.

Hickety, Pickety

Hickety, pickety, my black hen,
She lays eggs for gentlemen.
Gentlemen come every day
To see what my black hen does lay.

Pickety, peckity, my red hen,
Pecks at legs of gentlemen.
Gentlemen all run away
When my red hen comes out to lay.

Cackle, Cackle, Mother Goose

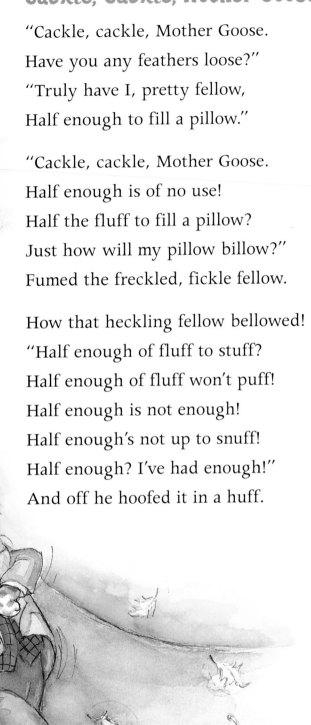

"Cackle, cackle, Mother Goose.
Have you any feathers loose?"
"Truly have I, pretty fellow,
Half enough to fill a pillow."

"Cackle, cackle, Mother Goose.
Half enough is of no use!
Half the fluff to fill a pillow?
Just how will my pillow billow?"
Fumed the freckled, fickle fellow.

How that heckling fellow bellowed!
"Half enough of fluff to stuff?
Half enough of fluff won't puff!
Half enough is not enough!
Half enough's not up to snuff!
Half enough? I've had enough!"
And off he hoofed it in a huff.

11

Doctor Foster Went to Gloucester

Doctor Foster went to Gloucester

In a shower of rain.

He stepped in a puddle,

Right up to his middle,

And never went there again.

Doctor Foster, frazzled, flustered,
In a flutter flew.
The spill caused a chill,
And the doctor fell ill
With a fever and flu—achoo!

Swan Swam Over the Sea

Swan swam over the sea.

Swim, swan, swim!

Swan swam back again.

Well swum, swan!

See slim swan swim.

Swim, slim swan!

See sleek swan swim.

Swim, sleek swan!

See swan swim well.

Well swum, swan!

See swan in sea swell.

Swell swim, swan!

See swan swoop, sway.

Swoop, swan, sway!

See swan swim away.

Stay, swan, stay!

14

Hippity Hop to the Barbershop

Hippity hop to the barbershop
To buy a stick of candy.
One for you and one for me,
And one for sister Annie.

Snippity snip—hear the barber clip.
It's time to get a shearing.
One for you and Annie, too,
But I'll be disappearing!

16

Fiddle Dee Dee

Fiddle dee dee, fiddle dee dee,
The fly has married the bumblebee.
They went to church,
And married was she.
The fly has married the bumblebee.

Fiddle dee dee, fiddle dee dee,
Oh what a joyful jubilee!
The guests all swarmed
And buzzed with glee
As the fair fly flew with the bumblebee.

Fiddle dee dee, fiddle dee dee,
The firefly and the flea agree
That snug as bugs
In rugs they'll be:
Mr. and Mrs. Bumblebee.

Peter Piper Picked a Peck of Pickled Peppers

Peter Piper picked a peck of pickled peppers.
A peck of pickled peppers Peter Piper picked.
If Peter Piper picked a peck of pickled peppers,
Then where's that peck of pickled peppers Peter Piper picked?

Peter Piper picked a peck of pickled peppers,
But Patty Piper picked a peck of pickled peppers quicker.
Into a pickled pepper pot she packed the peck of peppers,
For Patty was a quicker pickled pepper packer-picker.

Then Peter Piper ate the peck of peppers for his lunch.

He ate the pickled peppers, and he left no pepper speck.

A pickled pepper peckful he packed into his paunch,

But oh, poor Peter Piper puckered from that pickled peck!

Handy Spandy, Jack-a-dandy

Handy Spandy, Jack-a-dandy,
Loves plum cake and sugar candy.
He bought some at a grocer's store,
And out he came, hop, hop, hop.

Handy Spandy's cakes and candies,
Licorice, brownies, pecan sandies.
Can you believe he ate them all
And left not one drop, drop, drop?

Goppy, gloppy, creamy, sloppy
Custard pies so rich and soppy.
Some munchy, crunchy brittle bits,
A lollipop, pop, pop, pop.

Ooey, gooey, super gluey,
Tacky taffy, thick and chewy.
A dozen doughnuts filled with jam,
And icing on top, top, top.

23

Holy moly! Roly poly!
Fifteen cupcakes, twelve cannoli.
A hundred cherry jelly beans
In his mouth, plop, plop, plop.

Glummy, dummy, feeling crummy,
Too much sugar in his tummy.
Handy Spandy, Jack-a-dandy,
You really should stop!

Tweedledum and Tweedledee

Tweedledum and Tweedledee
Agreed to have a battle,
For Tweedledum, said Tweedledee,
Had spoiled his nice new rattle.
Just then flew by a monstrous crow
As black as a tar barrel,
Which frightened both our heroes so,
They quite forgot their quarrel.

The quaky pair had quite a scare.
Their knobby knees were knocking.
They quit their quibble then and there
And stopped their senseless squawking.
That startling crow pulled quite a stunt.
It left the Tweedles rattled,
And off our rabble-rousing runts
As quick as winks skedaddled.

25

Sippity Sup, Sippity Sup

Sippity sup, sippity sup,
Bread and milk from a china cup.
Bread and milk from a bright silver spoon
Made of a piece of the bright silver moon.
Sippity sup, sippity sup,
Sippity, sippity sup.

Sippity sop, sippity sop,
Soup in a bowl from a china shop.
Plenty of soup to sip and scoop.
Try not to slurp, but sip, your soup.
Sippity sop, sippity slop,
Slippity, sloppity slurp,

Burp!

Diddle, Diddle, Dumpling

Diddle, diddle, dumpling,
My son, John,
Went to bed
With his trousers on,
One shoe off
And one shoe on.
Diddle, diddle, dumpling,
My son, John.

Diddle, diddle, dumpling,
My son, John,
Should have left
Both shoes on.
Tickle those toesies
One by one!
Giggle, giggle, dumpling,
My son, John.

Wee Willie Winkie

Wee Willie Winkie
Runs through the town,
Upstairs and downstairs,
In his nightgown.
Rapping at the windows,
Crying through the lock,
"Are the children all in bed?
For now it's eight o'clock."

While other wee ones
Willingly dream,
Wild Wilma Winkless
Has no such scheme.
Whizzing like a whirlwind,
Wound up to the brink,
Wired and wide-eyed Wilma Winkless
Won't sleep one wee wink!

Well, was that fun? What do you think?
We hope that you were tickled pink.
But now this play has reached its end.
So toodleloo for now, our friend!

I hope that you enjoyed the show.
Now here's a treat before you go.
Why don't you take another look
For hidden pictures in the book?

The following objects are hidden in the illustrations:
    pages 6–7: balloon, bone, boot, butterfly, button
    page 9: watch, web, wheel, whistle, worm
    page 10: hamburger, hammer, hook, hoop, hose
    page 11: candle, carrot, cookie, crayon, cup
    pages 12–13: flashlight, flower, fly, football, fork
    pages 14–15: snail, sneaker, sock, spoon, straw
    pages 16–17: hamster, heart, horseshoe, hot dog, house
    pages 18–19: fan, feather, fish, flag, frog
    pages 20–21: peanut, pear, pencil, pickle, potato
    pages 22–23: daisy, deer, desk, dragon, dress
    page 25: tomato, toothbrush, triangle, tulip, turtle
    pages 26–27: scissors, spider, sponge, star, stick
    page 28: dinosaur, dish, doughnut, drum, duck
    pages 30–31: waffle, wagon, walrus, watermelon, whale

Dear Friends,

My love for nursery rhymes began when I was seven years old. I had just arrived in the United States from Poland and was given a big, beautiful Mother Goose collection. Speaking only Polish at the time, I soon began to learn English while I spent many magical hours immersed in that book. The sounds, rhythms, and playful language in the verses captivated me.

These days I am honored and delighted to be using those beloved nursery rhymes in the picture books I create. For this collection I selected poems with fun sounds and alliteration and extended them with a stanza or more of my own words, striving to maintain the integrity, plot, and meter of the original verses. Because of the nature of these poems, I decided to have Rufus and his friends act them out, adding to the fun of the "play" on words.

Children adore story time with cherished adults, and these poems are perfect for reading aloud together. So have fun, share giggles, and explore the wondrous world of words. I hope you enjoy reading these rhymes with your little ones as much as I enjoyed writing them for you!

Warm wishes,

Published by Charlesbridge
85 Main Street
Watertown, MA 02472
(617) 926-0329
www.charlesbridge.com

Illustrations done in watercolor, ink, and colored pencil
    on Fabriano 300-lb. watercolor paper (softpress)
Display type and text type set in Hip Hop and Apollo MT
Color separations by Chroma Graphics, Singapore
Printed and bound by Everbest Printing Company, Ltd.,
    through Four Colour Imports Ltd., Louisville, Kentucky
Production supervision by Brian G. Walker
Designed by Diane M. Earley

Library of Congress Cataloging-in-Publication Data
Trapani, Iza.
    Rufus and friends : rhyme time / extended and illustrated by Iza Trapani.
        p. cm.
        Summary: In this collection of tongue-twisting nursery rhymes, the reader is asked to find hidden objects in the illustrations.
        ISBN 978-1-58089-206-3 (reinforced for library use)
        ISBN 978-1-58089-207-0 (softcover)
        1. Nursery rhymes. 2. Children's poetry. [1. Nursery rhymes. 2. Tongue twisters. 3. Picture puzzles.] I. Title.
        PZ8.3.T686Rh 2008
        398.8—dc22   2007026200

Printed in China
(hc) 10 9 8 7 6 5 4 3 2 1
(sc) 10 9 8 7 6 5 4 3 2 1

Starring

Rufus

Lulu

Tucker

Stella

Mops